D0714834

For Snowy the survivor (seven lives left!) - P.B.
For Prinsi-Minsi - C.C.

First published 2022 by Macmillan Children's Books
an imprint of Pan Macmillan
The Smithson, 6 Briset Street, London, EC1M 5NR
EU representative: Macmillan Publishers Ireland Limited,
1st Floor, The Liffey Trust Centre, 117-126 Sheriff Street Upper,
Dublin 1, D01 YC43

Associated companies throughout the world
www.panmacmillan.com

ISBN 978-1-5290-1327-6

1 3 5 7 9 8 6 4 2

A CIP catalogue record for this book is available
from the British Library.
Printed in China

I am Cat!

Peter Bently
Chris Chatterton

Macmillan Children's Books

I am Cat.
Cat is me.

A most superior thing to be.

I like
stretchy-stretchy
paws.

I like
scratchy-scratchy
claws.

Cat is hungry.

Pad,
pad,
pad.

Human sleeping.
That's too bad.

Me-ow!
Me-ow!
Me-ow!
Me-ow!

Hello human!
This way now.

Purr-purr. Purr-purr.
Rumbling tum.

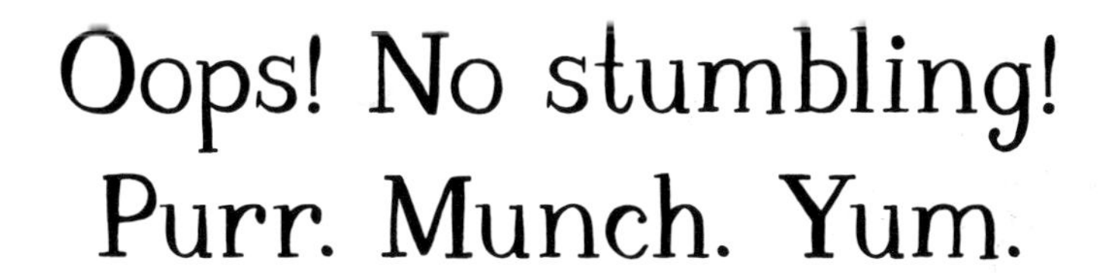

Oops! No stumbling!
Purr. Munch. Yum.

I am Cat.
I roam and prowl.
HISS! Intruder!
HISS! HISS!

YOWL!

Good.
No more intruders here.

I am Cat.
I have no fear.

Tiger, tiger stalking prey.
Hunting, hunting night and day.

Something moving. Mouse or frog?
Bird? Or toad? Or –

Next-door dog!

I am Cat. Bird I see.
Leopard, leopard up the tree.
Bird up. Cat up.
Bird up. Cat.
Bird. Cat.

Now I'll
catch you!
Drat.

I am Cat. Ignore the crowd.
Lion, lion fierce and proud.

Lick-lick.
Lick-lick.
Here.

And there.

Lick-lick.
Lick-lick.

Everywhere.

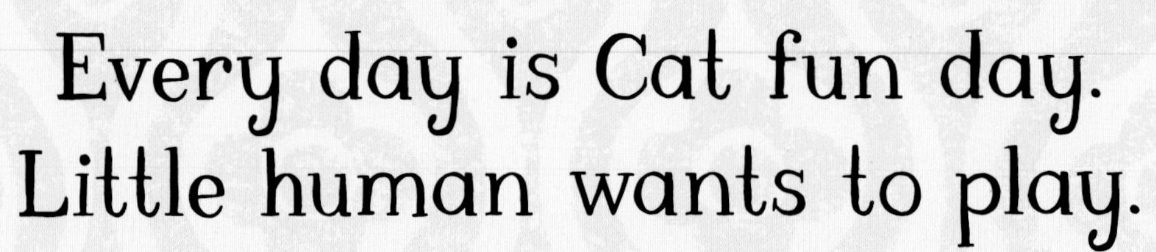

Every day is Cat fun day.
Little human wants to play.

This way. That way.
This way. That.

This way…

Gotcha!

I am Cat!

I am Cat.
I need nap.
Window?
Cupboard?

Dog bed?
Lap!

I am Cat. I love to hug.
Purr-purr.
Purr-purr.
Warm and
snug.

Little human strokey fur.
Ears. Chin. Tummy.
Purr-purr purr.

Me time.

Stretchy-stretch on mat.
Snooze till teatime.

I am Cat.